Best Wishes!

Sarah Sherman McGrail

2005

ISBN 0-9655925-2-9

To order more copies of this book
please contact the author
directly at:

Sarah Sherman McGrail

Cozy Harbor Press
P.O. Box 385
Southport, ME 04576

Phone: 207-633-7161
E-mail: ssherman@nnei.net

Printed by J.S. McCarthy Printers
Augusta, Maine

Design, art and production by
James A. Taliana,
Boothbay Harbor, Maine

COZY
HARBOR
PRESS

Dedication

To Jerry, Sherm, Jake, and Abby with Love.

Mama/Sarah

Acknowledgments

To Eliot and Marge Winslow

for technical assistance

and unwavering encouragement.

To Jim Taliana for his willingness

to try a new venture.

To Linda and Bob Jones –

Thank you for believing in me.

To Esme McTighe and Ellie Leo

for all your help.

The littlest Tugboat

By Sarah Sherman McGrail

Illustrated by James A. Taliana

Tommy Tugboat loved to work alongside
his big brothers, Charles, Gordon and Eliot
at the Bath Iron Works. Together, they pushed
and pulled with all their might, helping guide
great ships up and down the Kennebec River.

One day, the tugs' mother, Alice gathered them together and said, "Listen closely, children. I am going to teach you *The Song of Safe Passage*. Its words will help you find your way home if you ever get off course coming down the river."

Alice began to sing softly,
and the tugs scrambled to get
closer so they could hear the
lyrics to her song.

"**S**team on down the Sasanoa River.
Watch the current, boys. It will take you if it can.

Robinhood is ready if the seas are getting rocky.
MacMahan Island is a sure and steady friend.

Keep Goose Rock Passage on you port side, boys.
Steam across the Sheepscot River; home is just around the bend."

BATH

KENNEBEC RIVER

ARROWSIC ISLAND

SASANOA RIVER

HELL'S GATE

BACK RIVER

HELL'S GATE

WESTPORT ISLAND

MacMAHAN I.

GOOSE ROCK PASSAGE

BOSTON ISLAND

ISLE OF SPRINGS

SHEEPSCOT RIVER

INDIANTOWN I.

SAWYERS I.

HODGDON I.

BARTERS ISLAND

ROBINSON'S WHARF

OAK POINT

BACK RIVER

"Toot, toot your whistle so the bridge tender knows you're coming.

The swing-span opens quickly; traffic's back up once again.

There's Robinson's Wharf; her pilings are awaiting.

Tie up for the night, boys, and you're safely home again!"

Tommy Tugboat snuggled his fenders up against the strong pilings of the wharf. He was tired after a long day's work but took time to admire the stars shining above him as they twinkled in the moonlit sky.

"Did you have a big day at the shipyard?" His mother asked as she tucked him in. "Yes, I did Mom. I shifted a barge into place, and then I worked moving one of the big ships. Eliot and Charles were on the port side, and Gordon and I were on the starboard side."

His mother smiled and said, "It sounds like you've had a very big day. You'd better get some rest if you're going to keep up with your brothers tomorrow." She kissed him on the smokestack and went about the wharf making sure her other children were settled in for the night.

The next day was blustery and rough. A cold wind blew out of the northeast, and whitecaps whipped up on the tops of the waves. Tommy's brothers headed off to work despite the foul weather, but Tommy's mother took him aside and told him, "You must stay tied to the wharf today, dear. You aren't as experienced as your brothers are in stormy seas."

"Aw, Mom. You worry too much. Please, can't I go with Charles, Gordon and Eliot? I promise I'll listen to what they say, and I'll stick close beside them," Tommy begged. "No, Tommy. I've made up my mind. This kind of weather gets dangerous quickly for a little tug, and I think you should stay home with me," his mother explained.

Tommy was very disappointed and sulked all the way back to his piling. "I don't see why I can't go. I kept up with Gordon just fine yesterday," Tommy mumbled bitterly to himself.

"Squawk, why don't you slip your hawser and show them how big you are?" Sammy Seagull asked as he landed on top of Tommy's piling. "What do you mean?" Tommy replied, startled that someone had overheard him complaining. "Squawk, just what I said," coaxed Sammy. "If you're so big, why don't you steam up the river yourself and show them once and for all?"

Tommy thought for a moment, overlooking the fact that Sammy was a known troublemaker, and said, "You're right. I'll show them!"

Tommy gave his hawser a quick flick, and it jumped right off the bitt and onto his deck. He gave a toot toot of appreciation to Sammy for the idea and started to steam off on his way, bound and determined to show his mother that he was big enough for the job.

TOOT TOOT!

TOMMY

W

"I don't see what all the fuss was about," thought Tommy as he passed by Green Island with ease.

Once he got out of the lee of the island and hit the Sheepscot River, it was suddenly a different story. Waves crashed over his bow, and he struggled to stay in control as his hull was tossed to and fro by the mighty ocean. "This is too much for me!" Tommy nervously exclaimed. "Mom was right! I'd better get home before I get into real trouble."

Tommy quickly turned right full rudder, then steamed full ahead. Before long, he passed the Ink Bottle, and Tommy noticed an osprey had built a large nest atop the flashing navigational marker.

Bits and pieces of rope and moss hung out of the sturdy structure, and a mackerel wiggled in the seabird's talons as Tommy passed by.

The osprey seemed oblivious to the tugboat and gobbled his lunch up in a few greedy bites.

Despite the wind, Tommy heard lots of
yelling coming from Townsend Gut. He strained
to hear what the commotion was. Then, as he
rounded Oak Point, he saw the problem with
his own eyes. A large barge had broken free
from its anchors in a nearby cove and was
drifting towards the Southport Bridge.
High winds and strong currents aided its
progress, and no one seemed to know
how to stop it.

Tommy quickly radioed the bridge tender, "Southport Bridge, do you read me? Over."
"Tommy, is that you?" came back a relieved response. "Can you help us before the barge hits the bridge?" asked Dwight the bridge tender.

"I'll do my best," replied Tommy. "I'll need some help. Can someone come aboard?" asked the littlest tugboat.

"Sure thing Tommy. My brother Duane is here to man the bridge, so I'll go with you," replied Dwight. Tommy steamed past the barge and picked him up as he climbed down the framework of the bridge.

Tommy mustered all the strength his engines could turn out as he raced towards the approaching barge. "Put my hawser around the double towing bitt in the stern. When I give you the signal, jump onto the barge and secure the other end," instructed Tommy. Dwight nodded and prepared to leap aboard.

The wind was really screeching now, and Tommy found it difficult to stay alongside the barge. With one last burst of energy, Tommy revved his engines, and pushed his fenders into the barge. At that very moment, the bridge tender bounded aboard the runaway barge and put the hawser around a large bitt. The bridge was getting closer by the minute, and spectators had started to gather on the shoreline, anticipating a great disaster.

25

Tommy hastily charged full ahead, but the barge resisted with all its might. "You'll never stop me!" taunted the barge as it pulled Tommy backwards. "Come on, guys, give me all you've got!" Tommy shouted at the horsepower in his mighty diesel engine.

The strain on the hawser was great, but despite the load it carried, it didn't give way. Slowly but surely, the littlest tugboat started to pull the barge away from the bridge. A round of cheers could be heard from shore, led by Captain Eliot Winslow himself. Tommy couldn't help but look back over his stern once or twice at the appreciative crowd.

Once the barge was secure,
Tommy dropped Dwight off at
a nearby float and headed home
to Robinson's Wharf.
His mother was waiting there for him,
half-smiling, half-shaking her head.

"I don't know if I should hug you because I'm so proud or if I should punish you for disobeying me," huffed his exasperated mother. Tommy sheepishly steamed into his berth. "Oh, Mom! I know I shouldn't have gone out today, but if I hadn't, the barge surely would have taken out the bridge," replied Tommy.

Just then Charles, Gordon, and Eliot steamed into the cove.
"What's all the commotion?" Gordon asked. "Your brother is a hero,"
answered Alice as she explained the day's events.

"Three cheers for Tommy!" cried Eliot. "Hip, hip, hooray! Hip, hip, hooray!
Hip, hip, hooray! shouted the family of tugboats, as Tommy's smokestack
turned red with embarrassment.

Hip Hip Hooray!

From that day forward, Tommy went wherever his older brothers went. No job was too big or too small, and Alice never worried about the weather because she knew Tommy could handle himself. Sometimes the words <u>littlest</u> and <u>bravest</u> go hand in hand, don't you think?

THE END

The Littlest Tugboat
G L O S S A R Y

Tugboat-- A strongly-built, heavily-powered vessel used for towing or pushing other vessels.

Barge-- A vessel, without power used for transporting freight.

Smokestack-- A pipe for the escape of smoke or gasses from a combustion engine.

Fenders-- A piece of timber, bundle of rope, or rubber tires hung over the side of a vessel to lessen shock or prevent chafing.

Pilings-- A heavy timber, stake, or pole driven vertically into the ground or the bed of a river. Used to support buildings, wharfs, and for boats or tugboats to tie up to.

Bitt-- A strong post of wood or iron projecting (usually in pairs) above the deck of a ship. Used for securing cables or lines for towing.

Hawser-- A small cable or large rope used in mooring or towing a ship.

Anchor-- A device for holding boats or vessels in place.

Right Full Rudder-- A maximum right turn - 45 degrees.

Osprey-- A large hawk that feeds on fish. Commonly known in Maine as a fishhawk.

The Ink Bottle-- A flashing navigational marker located in Townsend Gut between Southport and Boothbay Harbor, Maine.

Robinson's Wharf-- A lobster-buying wharf and restaurant.

Bath Iron Works-- Builder of large Navy warships.

About the Author

Sarah Sherman McGrail is a Southport Island native. She was educated in the island's three-room schoolhouse, where her children currently attend, and is a student at the University of Maine at Augusta pursuing her B.A, in English. *The Littlest Tugboat* is Sarah's third publication. Her first two, *Southport: The War Years* and *Heroes Among Us*, recorded veterans' stories from the Second World War.

About the Illustrator

James (Jim) Taliana is a resident of Boothbay Harbor, Maine. He was born in Detroit, Michigan; and is an alumnus of the Center for Creative Studies (CCS) in Detroit where he majored in advertising and fine art. Jim worked at an ad agency for 28 years on accounts such as Cadillac, Whirlpool, FTD, Mr. Goodwrench, Kirsch and Dow. Then started his own design firm while teaching advertising at CCS until he and his wife Gloria moved to Maine in 2002.

Jim is represented by galleries in Michigan, North Carolina and Maine, and is in many private collections here and abroad.

About the Tugboats

The inspiration for The Littlest Tugboat came from Eliot and Marge Winslow's real life fleet of tugboats. They were a familiar sight to the author as she grew up on Southport Island, and they were often tied at the Winslows' other business, Robinson's Wharf. The big black **W** on their smoke stack was a welcome landmark to islanders as they crossed the green swing-span bridge.

Eliot's original fleet consisted of the *Argo*; Charlie Wade's *Balmy Days*; Samples Shipyard's *Jane*; and Mace Carter's *Hi-M*. Together the four vessels would guide large ships up and down the Sheepscot River. In 1972, the Winslows founded Sheepscot Pilots, a towboat company. Eliot and Marge bought the *Oscar Smith* and renamed her the *Alice Winslow* in memory of Eliot's mother. She was 96 feet long, had a 22-foot beam, a 1250 horsepower engine, and she was fast, able to steam up to 13 knots.

Over the years the *Marjory*, *Argonaut*, *Eliot*, *Peggy*, the second *Alice Winslow* (built new at Washburn and Doughty in East Boothbay, Maine, in 1991), and *Mini Winnie* were added to the fleet. Eliot and Marge also ran a successful tour boat business, taking passengers around Southport Island and up and down the Sheepscot River on the *Argo*. One day when it became quite evident that the tugboat business had really started to take off, Marge looked at Eliot and said, "You've either got to fish or cut bait!" That was all it took, and Eliot gave up 33 years of tour boat business for a life of tugboats.

Over the years, Winslow tugs docked ships at the Bath Iron Works and did various towboat jobs in Portland Harbor. Their biggest job ever was bringing two sound domes for B.I.W. back from Quebec, Canada. The domes were shaped like a whale's tail, and went under a ship's stem, acting as the eyes and ears of the ship to listen for enemy submarines. The sound domes were 60 feet long, 16 feet high and had a 20 foot beam. They were too large and heavy to be transported over the road or by train, so they had to be brought in by sea.

The Winslows' son David now runs the company under the name Winslow Marine. He is based out of Portland, Maine, and currently moves ships for B.I.W. He also operates a towing and barge service that transports equipment, lumber, and supplies. A new development in recent years has been the opportunity to do bunkering work, re-fueling ships at sea, and Winslow Marine participates in that part of the industry as well.

Color me!

Tommy tows the runaway barge away from the bridge.

Tommy and his mother talk about the days events.